The Tempest

Written by

John Dougherty

Illustrated by

Marcela Calderón

Collins

Cast of characters

Prospero – Duke of Milan and a powerful magician

Miranda – daughter of Prospero

Antonio – Miranda's uncle, Prospero's brother

King Alonso of Naples

*Sebastian –
King Alonso's
brother*

*Ferdinand –
King Alonso's
son*

*Gonzalo –
adviser to King
Alonso*

*Caliban –
an island-dweller*

*Ariel –
a magical spirit
who becomes
Prospero's servant*

*The bosun –
a crewman on
the king's ship*

Chapter 1

Miranda's father and her uncle Antonio were arguing again.

"For goodness sake, Prospero," Antonio was saying. "Just sign the papers, and I'll go."

"Yes," snapped her father, "but before long you'll be back, *again*. You'll interrupt my studies, *again*. And it'll be about some pointless bits of paper, again."

"They may seem pointless to *you*," Antonio said. "But these are the laws by which your people must live. You *are* the Duke of Milan – or had you forgotten?"

Prospero's voice became horribly calm. "No, Antonio,"
he said. "I haven't forgotten. And nor have I forgotten that
I put you in charge of the day-to-day running of the city.
So that I can continue my studies in peace!"

The sudden shouting made Miranda, in her hiding-place
on the stairs, flinch. But Antonio simply said, "Well,
dear brother, since you are the duke, the laws must have
your signature. Unless you'd like to make *me* the duke,
so *I* can sign them? Not that I have any desire to be duke,
of course. It looks like *such* hard work."

Prospero snatched the bundle of papers from
Antonio's hand. Barely glancing at
them, he scribbled his signature
on page after page.
"There!" he said angrily.
"Now, surely, the city has
enough laws!"

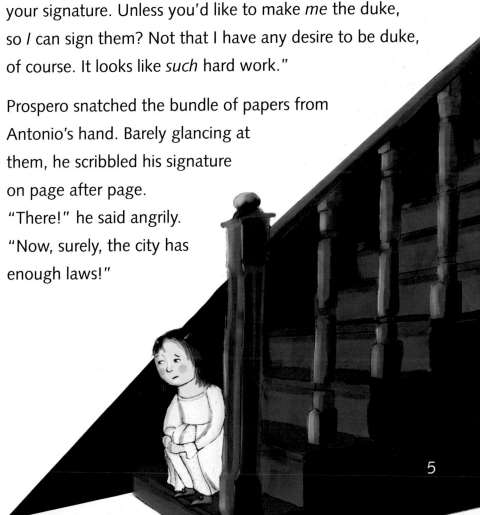

There was something mocking about the way that Antonio bowed and turned to leave. Just as he reached the door, he looked back. "By the way, Prospero – what exactly are you studying? I'd love to know what's *so* much more important than ruling the city?"

Prospero said nothing. But as Antonio left, Miranda saw her father stretch out his hand, and mutter under his breath.

Without anybody touching it, the door slammed.

Chapter 2

Loud shouting woke Miranda. She lay very still in her bed. She could hear several voices, and above them, her father's, roaring in fury.

The door to her room burst open. A soldier stepped inside and snatched her up. Miranda burst into frightened tears.

"Miranda!" It was her father's voice, from the floor below. Then came another voice that she recognised:

"Behave, Prospero, and she'll not be harmed."

It was her uncle Antonio.

The soldier carried her downstairs; her father reached out and took her. Miranda buried her face in his shoulder and sobbed.

Her father held her gently,
but his voice, as he spoke to
his brother, was harsh.

"What do you mean by
coming here in the middle of
the night with foreign soldiers,
Antonio? If I'm not mistaken,
they belong to the King
of Naples!"

"Indeed they do," said
Antonio smoothly. "These are
King Alonso's men."

"How dare you bring them
to my city?" Prospero
demanded. "You know that
King Alonso is greedy for power! He wants nothing more
than to bring Milan under his control!"

Antonio smiled coldly. "His wish is granted, then. The Duke
of Milan is King Alonso's servant now."

Miranda, still sobbing, felt her father stiffen. "I will never
serve that man!"

"No, Prospero, I know," said Antonio. "And you won't have to. Because you're no longer the Duke of Milan. I am."

* * * * * * * *

The rest of that night passed in a blur for Miranda. Wrapped in her father's cloak, she was carried outside, and into a carriage. She fell asleep then; and when she awoke, she was in a bed that swayed gently with the rocking of the sea. Her father was sitting in a chair nearby.

A sad-looking stranger stood by the door. "My name is Gonzalo," he told Miranda. "I must ask you both to come with me."

Gonzalo led them out on deck. Miranda realised they were on a tall ship, far out at sea. A small boat was being made ready to lower over the side.

"So, Gonzalo," Prospero said. "You are to cast us adrift?"

Gonzalo nodded unhappily. "Those are my orders. But I have made sure this little boat is well supplied."

Prospero looked into the boat, and his expression softened. "Food and water," he said. "Blankets and clothing. Everything we need to survive. And in these boxes…?"

He lifted the lid of one, and Miranda was amazed to see that – just for a moment – he smiled. "My books," he said, in a tone of wonder.

They were her father's books of magic. This, Miranda knew, was what Prospero had been studying for all those years.

Gonzalo nodded again. "I hope you will find an island where you can continue your studies in peace."

"Thank you," said Prospero. "Though your master is my enemy, Gonzalo, you have shown yourself to be my friend."

They shook hands. Then Prospero and Miranda climbed into the little boat, and the sailors lowered it over the side of the tall ship.

Chapter 3

Days later, the little boat washed up on an uncharted island. They built a simple shelter to keep them dry, and a fire to keep animals away, and they slept.

The days that followed were taken up with improving their shelter, exploring, and searching for food. One morning, Miranda entered a small grove of trees. A noise made her turn, and she gasped in fright.

Staring at her with wide eyes, and shuffling towards her, was a hideous, shaggy-haired boy. Miranda screamed. The boy stopped, confused.

Miranda stepped back. "Who are you?" she asked.

The boy babbled at her. It sounded as though he were speaking some foreign language badly, like a much younger child. But one word was clear:

"Caliban."

"Caliban," Miranda repeated. "Is that your name? Caliban?"

Caliban grinned a twisted, monstrous grin. "Caliban!" he repeated.

By the time they found Prospero, Miranda had taught Caliban her name, and that the bright light in the sky was the sun, and that the creatures that flew above them were birds. And Caliban had shown her a spring of fresh water.

It soon became clear that Caliban had been alone on the island. He was glad of their company – particularly Miranda's. Wherever she went he was there, eager to help her – or just to be with her. He showed them where to find food. Day by day he helped them to turn their rough shelter into a home. As they worked, Miranda and her father taught him to speak.

Then Prospero made a discovery of his own.

Caliban was showing them
a part of the island they hadn't
seen before, where fruit
trees grew and wild deer
roamed, when Prospero
heard something.

"Shhh!" he commanded.
"What's that sound?"

Miranda looked at
him, puzzled. "I can't
hear anything," she
said. "Except for
the birdsong, and
the sound of the sea."

Caliban just shrugged.

Prospero said nothing more,
but as they walked, he listened,
and the sound grew louder. It sounded like someone
crying; but clearly neither Miranda nor Caliban could
hear it. As soon as he could, Prospero left them
gathering fruit and firewood, and set off in search of
the source of the sound.

It wasn't long before he came
to a lone pine tree standing on
a hillside. From inside the tree
came the most pitiful sobbing
Prospero had ever heard.

"Who are you?" he demanded.
"*What* are you?"

The sobbing stopped, suddenly,
and an amazed voice said,
"My name's Ariel. I'm a spirit –
a creature of magic, invisible to
humans. How is it that you can
hear me?"

"I'm a sorcerer," Prospero replied
proudly. "I can do many things
that other humans cannot."

Ariel's voice was eager.
"Then… can you free me?
I have been trapped in this tree
for 12 long years, imprisoned by
the magic of an evil witch!"

"I'll release you," Prospero said,
"if you'll be my servant."

"Gladly, master!" came the voice
in reply.

Prospero held out his wooden
staff and muttered some words
of enchantment. The great tree
split in two. There, hovering in
the air, Prospero saw a shimmering
creature, like a child made of air
and light. The spirit bowed.

"I'm your servant, my lord," Ariel
said. "Command me."

Chapter 4

Prospero kept Ariel a secret from Miranda – and especially from Caliban. Prospero had never completely trusted the monstrous boy.

Life on the island went on. The days turned into weeks, and the weeks into years. Before long Caliban was a young man – an ugly, monstrous man. And Miranda was growing into a beautiful young woman.

One day, Miranda was working in the house when Caliban entered, an odd look on his face.

"Miranda" he began, and then stopped.

"Yes?" Miranda asked uneasily.

Caliban lunged awkwardly across the room and tried to take her hand; she snatched it away.

"Miranda!" he cried. "I love you! I want to marry you!"

Miranda was horrified. She'd always tried to be kind to Caliban, but the idea of marrying him made her feel ill. She tried not to show her disgust, but her face betrayed her.

Caliban saw. Caliban understood. And Caliban was humiliated.

"You think I'm not good enough!" he bellowed. "You think you're better than me!" In fury he swung his arms madly. His elbow caught a vase, smashing it against a wall. Miranda screamed.

Caliban was too angry to notice. "This is my island!" he yelled. "I shared it with you! I showed you where to find food! *I kept you alive!*" He stamped wildly on the floor, each stamp a step that brought him closer to Miranda.

Miranda, terrified, backed against the wall. "Caliban…" she tried to say; but her voice failed her and all that came out was a whisper of air.

"*You owe me your life!*" Caliban shrieked, his fists thrashing wildly and clumsily; furniture splintered beneath them. Miranda screamed again.

Behind Caliban, the door burst open. Prospero stood in the doorway, his face furious. "Caliban!" he roared.

Caliban was too enraged even to hear him. He took another step; Miranda could smell his foul breath and feel it on her face…

Prospero stretched out his hand and muttered something. Caliban crumpled to the floor, groaning in sudden agony.

"Spirit, hold him!" commanded Prospero. He stepped forward and stood over the monstrous man. "Enough!" he said, and Caliban lay still.

"I might have known," hissed Prospero.. "No good can come from taking in a witch's child! I treated you as my son, and this is how you behave! You will no longer live here as part of my family. Instead you'll be my slave! Spirit, remove him!"

Miranda watched in amazement as Caliban was lifted to his feet by invisible hands and pushed out of the door.

"Take him to the cave near the white rocks!" Prospero ordered his invisible servant. "He'll live there from now on!"

Miranda slumped to the floor with relief. Prospero strode across the room and stood over her.

"It's all right, my child," he said. "You're safe now."

Spring turned into summer, and summer into autumn.
Autumn became winter, and winter became spring.
The years rolled by. And then, one night, a ship came.

Prospero saw the light of its lanterns, shining in
the distance, and his magic told him who was aboard.
Standing on a high cliff, he stretched his hand out towards
the ship, and began to mutter.

The sky grew darker. The waves began to roll and swell. From nowhere came a mighty wind. The clouds burst; cold, hard, heavy rain pounded the ship. Lightning flashed; thunder boomed. The ship was tossed high, like a toy, and swept low, the mountainous sea driving it towards the island.

Prospero smiled grimly. "Ariel!" he said. "That ship carries Alonso, King of Naples. His son and his brother are with him. My treacherous brother Antonio and my noble friend Gonzalo are also aboard. Fly to it and make the passengers think it's sinking. Bring them safely to my island and bring the king's son to me. Go!"

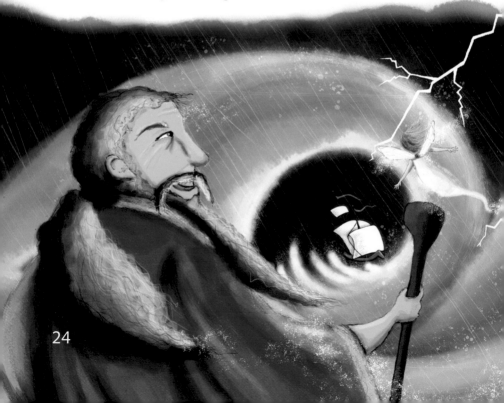

On the deck of the ship, all was chaos.

"Take in the topsail!" yelled the bosun, battling against the wind.

"Bosun!" shouted King Alonso, "where's the ship's master?"

"Get below!" ordered the bosun, as lightning flashed around him. "You're getting in the way!"

"Remember who you're talking to!" Gonzalo shouted, above the roaring of the storm.

"When the storm pays attention to the king, so will I!" the bosun bawled. "Now shut up and get below!"

"Shut up yourself, peasant!" bellowed Sebastian, the king's brother.

"*Get to work or get below!*" the bosun yelled, hauling in the sails.

"Aha!" thought Ariel. "The King and his men are adding to the confusion. Let's see what I can do to help them!"

Faster than light Ariel flew, from bow to stern; from port to starboard; from deck to mast to wheel. Flames flared and noises boomed and crashed in the spirit's wake, until it seemed to the terrified passengers that the whole world was ablaze. There came a dreadful cracking, splitting sound; and the sailors froze in fear.

26

"The ship's breaking up!" shouted Ferdinand, the king's son. With that, he leapt into the sea.

"Ferdinand!" shouted King Alonso, plunging in after him.

Whether to help the king, or to flee the ship, the rest of the king's men followed.

Chapter 6

"Ferdinand!" shouted the king above the raging of
the tempest; but there was no sign of his son. The sea
crashed around him. He felt himself lifted up; dragged
down; lifted up again. A huge wave seized him; hurled him
through the air; dashed him against something hard…

When King Alonso woke, the storm was over. He was lying
on a sandy shore. Next to him were his brother Sebastian,
Duke Antonio of Milan and the faithful Gonzalo.

Ariel had already gone. Faster than the wind, the spirit was gathering others from the sea, and scattering them around the island. Ferdinand, the king's son, woke to find himself alone upon the beach. From somewhere nearby, he thought he could hear music. Drawn by the enchanting sound, he rose and followed it.

On the dunes above, Prospero and Miranda looked down at him. Prospero, of course, could see Ariel leading the prince along, but Miranda could only see Ferdinand. It seemed to her that she'd never seen anyone so handsome.

"Father," she said. "Look! How wonderful! Is that a magical creature of some kind?"

"No, Miranda," her father replied. "That is a man."

"But he looks so different from you and Caliban!"

Prospero laughed softly. "He's much younger than me; and few people look like Caliban."

"But where did he come from?" Miranda asked.

"From the ship that was caught in the storm just now," Prospero told her.

Ariel, still singing the magical song, flew up to join Prospero. Ferdinand, following the sound, looked up.He saw a tall, bearded man in a shimmering cloak – and a young woman who, he thought, was the most beautiful person he'd ever seen. He stood, amazed, as they came down to meet him; and then he bowed.

"My lady," he said, "forgive me, but… are you human, or a magical creature of some kind?"

Miranda smiled. "I'm not magical," she said. She looked at him shyly, thinking again how handsome he was. "I'm human, like you."

30

Prospero looked from one to the other, and he was pleased. "Ariel!" he said, in a magical whisper that only the spirit could hear. "Well done! They're falling in love with each other already!"

"You're pleased with that, my lord?" Ariel asked.

"I am!" Prospero replied, in the same magical whisper. "This is why I asked you to bring him here. Because of what the King of Naples did to me, Miranda will never rule Milan. But if she marries Ferdinand, one day she'll be Queen of Naples!"

"That seems fair, my lord!" said Ariel.

"However…" Prospero went on, "I don't want to make it too easy for him. People value most what they have worked for. I think I should make Ferdinand work hard to earn Miranda's hand in marriage. If he doesn't want to, it will prove that he doesn't truly love her." To Ferdinand he said, "Who are you, and what are you doing on my island?"

"Father!" Miranda said. "Why are you sounding so angry?"

"Because this man is a spy!" Prospero said accusingly.

"I'm not a spy," Ferdinand said. "I'm Ferdinand, the Prince of Naples." And then his face grew sad, as he added, "And now, perhaps, I am the King of Naples. I think my father may have drowned when the ship was wrecked."

Miranda put out a hand to comfort him, but Prospero stopped her. "A likely story" he said. "You're a spy, come to steal this island from me!"

"No!" protested Ferdinand.

"Father, please!" Miranda said. "Why are you being so horrible?"

"I might just throw you in prison," said Prospero.

Ferdinand looked defiantly at him. "I could cope with that," he said, "if you just let me see your beautiful daughter every day through the prison bars!"

"Well," said Prospero, "we'll see about that. Come with me!" And to Ariel, he whispered, "Go, my servant, and find out what the other visitors to our island are doing."

Hidden in the dunes nearby, Caliban burned with silent anger. He, too, could see that Miranda was falling in love with Ferdinand. And he could see that Prospero was letting it happen.

Chapter 7

King Alonso would not be comforted, yet Gonzalo kept trying. "Your majesty, it's like a miracle! You, your brother, Duke Antonio – you've all survived…"

"He doesn't give up, does he?" Sebastian whispered.

"Silly old fool" Antonio agreed.

"Thank you, Gonzalo – but that's enough." The king's voice was sad and quiet. "I cannot be cheerful. My son has drowned."

"We don't know that, your majesty!" Gonzalo protested. "He's a good swimmer; he may have…"

"No, Gonzalo," Alonso said firmly. "He's drowned. I'm sure of it."

"Well, if he has, it's your own fault!"
Sebastian interrupted. "We wouldn't
have been on that ship if
it wasn't for you! We all
begged you to stay at
home, but would you listen
to us? No! And now see
what's happened!"

"My lord Sebastian,"
Gonzalo said, "can
you not see how sad
the king is? This is not
the time for accusations!"

Sebastian and Antonio scowled.

None of them could see that Ariel was standing
amongst them, listening to their bickering and growing
quite tired of Sebastian and Antonio. "I don't like these
two," the spirit thought. "I don't like the way they whisper
and mutter to one another." With that, Ariel began to
sing again, a different song but equally enchanting.

Moments later, both Gonzalo and the king were
fast asleep.

"This is strange," Sebastian said. "Why should they both fall asleep at once? I don't feel sleepy at all."

"Me neither" agreed Antonio. "Which could be very lucky for you, Sebastian. This is your big chance!"

"What do you mean?" Sebastian asked, not entirely innocently.

"Let me put it like this," Antonio said. "Ferdinand, the king's son, is dead, yes?"

"I'm afraid so" Sebastian agreed. "It's terribly sad." He did not sound sad in the least.

"So if Alonso were to die tragically in his sleep" Antonio continued, "who would be king after him?"

"Why – as the king's brother, I suppose that would be me" Sebastian said, in a tone of pretend surprise.

"And what do you think about that?" Antonio persisted.

Sebastian rubbed his chin thoughtfully. "Tell me, Antonio" he said. "Do you ever feel guilty about what you did to your brother Prospero?"

Antonio grinned cruelly. "Not in the slightest," he said. "I'm glad I took his place. And with the help of my sword you can take your brother's place – while *your* sword makes sure Gonzalo never tells anyone."

Sebastian's smile was just as cruel. "Let's do it" he said. "Draw your sword. Your new king will reward you!"

"Let's draw our swords together," Antonio said.

Ariel had heard enough. Prospero would be angry if Alonso and Gonzalo were killed. But he would be pleased to hear what Ariel had discovered. Quickly, the spirit knelt, and sang a new song in Gonzalo's ear.

Just at the moment that Sebastian and Antonio drew their swords, Gonzalo awoke with a start, and a cry that woke the king.

"What's happening?" King Alonso demanded. "Why are your swords drawn?"

"We… we heard a noise," said Sebastian.

"Did you hear it, Gonzalo?" asked the king doubtfully.

"I heard *something,*" Gonzalo said. "I think we should move on."

"Perhaps we should," said King Alonso.

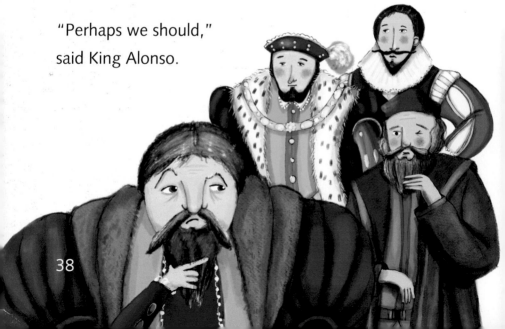

Chapter 8

Meanwhile, Ferdinand was working hard. Prospero had not imprisoned him as he had threatened, but he'd ordered him to move and stack thousands of heavy logs.

Ferdinand found he didn't mind the task. As he worked, he thought of Miranda, and the memory of her smile cheered him.

And as he lifted the next log, he looked up and saw her.

"Please don't work so hard, Ferdinand," she said. "Let me help you! I'll carry the logs for a while."

"Never!" said Ferdinand. "But stay here, and you'll give me enough strength to do my work. I've never met anyone as perfect as you."

Miranda smiled. "I've never met anyone," she said. "Except for you, and my father, and Caliban. But now that I *have* met you, I don't mind if I never meet anyone else."

"So," thought Prospero who, magically invisible, had been watching the whole time. "They really do love each other. I'm glad. Now, I must hurry. I have much to do!"

Prospero was not the only secret onlooker. Hidden behind the enormous log pile, Caliban watched, his heart full of hatred.

He saw how Miranda smiled at this stranger, Ferdinand. He hated her now, because he knew she would never smile that way at him. He hated Ferdinand, too.

But most of all, Caliban hated Prospero. He hated him for allowing his precious daughter to fall in love with Ferdinand. He hated him for making himself lord of the island. He hated Prospero for enslaving him.

Angry and alone, he made for his cold cave, his thoughts full of revenge.

Elsewhere on the island, King Alonso and his followers were lost.

"My old bones are aching, your majesty," Gonzalo said. "I'm sorry, but I need to rest."

"I don't blame you," Alonso said, sitting down. "I'm exhausted too."

"Good" Antonio muttered to Sebastian. "If they're exhausted, they'll sleep soundly. And we can make sure they never wake up again."

"Yes" agreed Sebastian. "Let's take care of them tonight."

"No" thought Prospero, who, still invisible, had come to stand among them. "You won't be 'taking care' of anyone." He mumbled under his breath, stretching out his hand, and the air filled with mysterious, magical music.

"What's that?" the king cried, leaping to his feet. Though all of them could hear the music, none of them could see where it was coming from.

"Now" Prospero thought, "to teach you a lesson. First I'll amaze and confuse you. Then, when your minds are filled with wonder, I'll remind you of your own wickedness." He stretched out his hands, summoning spirits, and the spirits came.

They made themselves visible to the astounded travellers, taking on strange and astonishing shapes. A great table appeared, filled with a wonderful banquet. With gestures, the spirits invited the king and his men to eat; and then they vanished, and all was quiet. The men stared at the feast before them.

"Should we eat?" asked Sebastian. "I'm starving!"

The king shrugged. "What's there to lose?" he said, and reached out his hand.

There was a sudden
crash of thunder and
a flash of lightning.
A dreadful winged creature
appeared on the table
in front of them, and
the food vanished.
King Alonso cried out in
alarm, and stepped back.

"This feast is not for wicked men!"
the creature screeched. "And you three,"
it continued, pointing a sharp claw in turn at King
Alonso, Sebastian and Antonio, "are most wicked!"

The three drew their swords. The creature laughed.

"Your swords cannot harm me!" it said. "Now, listen:
you three took Prospero's dukedom, and cast him
and his innocent daughter adrift at sea. For that,
King Alonso, the sea has taken your son from you.
It has left you all here upon this island. The only
way you can avoid a horrible death here, is to prove
that in your hearts you are genuinely sorry for all
your wickedness!"

There was another clap of thunder, and the creature vanished. Or, rather, it became invisible. Only the invisible Prospero could see its true shape – that of his servant Ariel.

"Well done, Ariel," he whispered.

King Alonso turned pale. "It's my fault that Ferdinand has drowned!" he cried. "I should never have plotted with you, Antonio. I should never have sent my soldiers to help you overthrow Prospero. All I cared about was becoming more powerful. All I cared about was making my kingdom greater!" He fell to his knees, tears flowing down his cheeks. "But my son is worth more than my entire kingdom – and because of my greed, I've lost him for ever. My poor Ferdinand has been punished for my wicked actions, and I'll live with this guilt for the rest of my life!"

Prospero, still invisible, smiled. "Ariel!" he commanded, "make sure Caliban is up to no mischief, and then come back here and listen to what the king's saying! I want to make sure he truly regrets his wickedness!"

Chapter 9

It was later that evening that Ariel returned to Prospero's home.

"Tell me," Prospero said, "do you think the king is truly sorry for taking my dukedom and casting Miranda and me out of Milan?"

"I do, master" said Ariel. "I've never seen anyone so sad."

"Then bring him and his companions here" Prospero said.

It wasn't long before Ariel, singing the magical song, returned. Moments later, King Alonso, Gonzalo, Sebastian and Antonio arrived.

"What place is this?" King Alonso asked as they entered. "Who are… But I know you! It's not possible!"

Prospero bowed. "It's both possible and true, your majesty. I am Prospero, and I welcome you. And you, Gonzalo, my old friend." Then, in a whisper that only they could hear, he added to Sebastian and Antonio, "You two are less welcome. If I wanted, I could tell the king what traitors you are!" Then as the two stared in frightened astonishment, he added, "But I won't. As long as you change your ways."

"Prospero," King Alonso said, "if it's really you, I can only beg your forgiveness, and swear to make you Duke of Milan once more. But how did you come to this terrible island where… where I lost my son?"

"And where you have found him again!" said Prospero, drawing back a curtain.

King Alonso gasped as he saw, in the room behind
the curtain, his son, playing chess with a beautiful young
woman. The two were clearly in love with each other.

It took King Alonso a moment to find his voice again.
Then he cried, "Ferdinand!"

Ferdinand looked up, and leapt to his feet. "Father!"
he said, and rushed to him. "I thought you were dead."

"I thought you were dead, too!" said King Alonso in astonishment. "But… who's this?"

"Oh." Ferdinand blushed. "Father, this is the woman I'm going to marry. Beautiful Miranda, daughter of Prospero. Will you give us your blessing?"

King Alonso laughed out loud. "I will," he said. "How fitting that my son and Prospero's daughter will one day rule both Naples and Milan, as king and queen, together. I hope," he added seriously, "that this will in some small way help to make amends for my wicked behaviour all those years ago."

"And who's this?" cried Gonzalo, as someone else came in, led by the magical music. It was the ship's bosun, who looked as amazed as any of them.

"What?" cried the king. "Were the crewmen washed ashore, too?"

"Better than that, your majesty," said the sailor. "I still don't understand it, but soon after you and your men left the ship, the storm died down and we found ourselves in a bay, with the ship whole and ready to sail for home!"

"Are you pleased, master?" Ariel asked.

"Very pleased, my Ariel," Prospero whispered. "Well done. And now for Caliban."

It was only minutes later that Ariel led Caliban in.

Caliban trembled. "Please," he said, "don't let your spirits torment me."

Prospero looked down at him. "Your heart is full of hatred and wickedness, Caliban. I know you've wanted to kill me since that day years ago that you attacked my daughter. I know you would have tried, many times, if my spirits had not kept me safe. Should I treat you as you would have treated me?" Then, as Caliban began to plead, he went on, "Or should I treat you as King Alonso has treated me? He has restored my dukedom. Tomorrow, I'll sail away from this island. And as Milan has been given back to me, so I will give the island back to you. Now go, back to your cave, and dream of tomorrow."

Finally, in a magical whisper that nobody else could hear, he added, "And you, Ariel, have served me well. But when I return to Milan I'll give up magic and instead work to be the best duke I can be. So tomorrow, I'll set you free."

The next morning, Miranda stood on the deck of the great ship as the crew pulled up the anchor. Behind her, Ferdinand's uncle Sebastian and her uncle Antonio stood in guilty silence. Nearby, her father talked happily with King Alonso and his old friend Gonzalo.

Beside her stood Ferdinand. She smiled at him and, taking his hand, looked back at the island for the last time.

On the shoreline, something moved. She recognised the shape of Caliban – king of his little island at last, and perhaps truly happy for the first time in his life.

Above her, in the sky, and unseen by anyone except Prospero, Ariel disappeared into the clouds.

And as a gentle wind picked up, the ship set sail for Miranda's new home.

Caliban's Island

Ideas for reading

Written by Clare Dowdall, PhD
Lecturer and Primary Literacy Consultant

Reading objectives:
- identify and discuss themes in writing
- prepare (versions of) plays to read aloud and to perform, showing understanding through intonation, tone and volume so that the meaning is clear to an audience
- draw inferences such as inferring characters' feelings, thoughts and motives from their actions, and justifying inferences with evidence

Spoken language objectives:
- participate in discussions, presentations, performances, role play, improvisations and debates

Curriculum links: Geography – place knowledge; Art and design – use of materials

Resources: modelling/junk material, art materials for mask making, ICT

Build a context for reading

- Show children the image on the front cover. Ask children what a tempest is and what happens during one.

- Discuss why authors might use a tempest in a setting for a story or play. Help children to think about what it might represent in the story.

- Explain that this story is based on a famous play by William Shakespeare written 400 years ago. Gather information about Shakespeare and his plays.

Understand and apply reading strategies

- Turn to pp2–3. Discuss what each character might be like and what kind of voice they would have, based on the images and descriptions provided.